A Note from Lucy Daniels

Dear readers,

I'm so excited that Hodder Children's Books is publishing new editions of your favourite titles in the Animal Ark Pets series.

I know from your letters how much you enjoy sharing Mandy and James's love of animals. As you can tell, I'm a huge fan of animals myself and can't imagine a day when I will ever want to stop writing about them.

Happy reading!

With very best wishes,

Lucy

LUCY DANIELS

ANIMAL ARK PETS

Hamster Hotel

Hodder
Children's
Books

a division of Hodder Headline Limited

Special thanks to Sue Welford
Thanks also to C. J. Hall, B. Vet. Med., M.R.C.V.S. for reviewing
the veterinary information contained in this book

Animal Ark is a trademark of Working Partners Ltd
Copyright © 1996 Working Partners Ltd
Created by Working Partners Limited, London W6 0QT
Original series created by Ben M. Baglio
Illustrations copyright © 1996 Paul Howard
Cover illustration by Chris Chapman

First published in Great Britain in 1996 by Hodder Children's Books

This edition published in 2006 by Hodder Children's Books

For more information about Animal Ark,
please contact www.animalark.co.uk

1

A Catalogue record for this book is available from the British Library

ISBN 0 340 91785 7

Contents

Contents

1

A visitor at Lilac Cottage

"Mandy Hope, did you hear what I said?" Mrs Todd was standing right beside Mandy's school desk.

Mandy looked up at her teacher. She had been miles away. Today was the day that her grandmother's friend Mary was bringing her hamster to stay at Lilac Cottage, the house where Gran lived.

Mandy's grandparents were going to look after the hamster for a week while Mary was away on holiday and Mandy just couldn't wait to meet him.

"Oh, sorry, Mrs Todd," she said. "Er . . . no I didn't."

"What's the heaviest land animal in the world, next to the elephant, Mandy?"

The class were having a quiz and it was Mandy's turn to answer a question.

"Oh," Mandy said. "A rhinoceros."

You could ask Mandy anything about animals and she almost always knew the answer.

Mrs Todd nodded. "Good. Well done, Mandy!"

Mandy glanced up at the clock. Nearly three o'clock. Almost time to go home. Better still, it was half-term. She and her best friend, James Hunter, would have a whole week to spend with the hamster. James was a year younger than Mandy and loved animals almost as much as she did.

James had two pets. A Labrador puppy named Blackie and a cat called Benji.

Mandy would have loved to have a pet too, but her parents were both vets and were too busy looking after other people's animals to have pets of their own.

Mandy wanted to be a vet like her parents one day. She longed to help out with the sick animals at their surgery, Animal Ark, but knew she would have to wait until she was older.

When school had finished, Mandy helped Mrs Todd take Terry and Jerry, the class gerbils, out to her car. Mrs Todd was going to care for them at her house during the holiday.

Mandy said goodbye to Mrs Todd, then ran to meet James who was waiting by the school gate. They always went home together.

"Today's hamster day!" Mandy zipped up her coat against the cold wind.

James pushed his glasses on to the bridge of his nose. "I hadn't forgotten," he said. "When can I come and see him?"

"Mum said I could go straight to Gran's

after school," Mandy said. "You could come with me now if you like."

"Will your gran mind?" James asked.

"Of course she won't," said Mandy.

"Great!" said James, hurrying to keep up. "Let me just tell Mum where I'm going."

He ran on ahead to his house.

"Don't be long," Mandy called. "And better not bring Blackie this time – he might frighten the hamster."

James disappeared into his house.

Mandy waited for him by the front gate. Suddenly a black nose pushed the back door open and Blackie came scampering out. James followed soon after.

"Blackie!" James shouted. "Come back."

Blackie threw himself at Mandy, all big paws and wagging tail. Mandy laughed and gave him a cuddle. Blackie rolled over on his back with his legs in the air so Mandy could tickle his tummy.

James caught up with them and grabbed the puppy's collar. "Blackie, *when* will you learn to do as you're told?" He shook the puppy gently and scolded him. "He's learned to open the door," James explained to Mandy.

"So I see," she chuckled.

Blackie stood up and began licking her face. Mandy gave him another hug. "You're a very clever dog," she said.

"Yes, he is, but when is he going to behave?" said James.

"Never, by the looks of it." Mandy pushed Blackie gently away. "You'll have to take him to proper puppy training classes."

"Dad's already taken him," James told her as he hauled Blackie back into the house. "But he caused a riot."

Mandy chuckled. "A riot?"

"Yes. He ran off with the trainer's whistle, pinched the biscuits they were going to have at break time and got hold of a lady's scarf and tore it to bits. Dad won't take him again."

"I'm not surprised." Mandy burst out laughing. "One of our holiday jobs will have to be some serious training with Blackie," she said.

James looked glum. "We can try," he said. "But I don't hold out much hope – he hasn't improved much since the last time we tried."

Mandy skipped ahead as they made their way across the village green. It was a damp afternoon, with a hint of drizzle in the wind. "Come on, I can't wait to see the hamster!"

Grandad was busy in the garden of Lilac Cottage, pruning back the shrubs. The sleeves of his old gardening jumper were pushed up to the elbows. There was a wheelbarrow full of twigs and leaves on the path. Mandy pushed past it and ran to give him a hug.

"Come to see Frisky, the hamster?" Grandad asked.

"Yep. I've brought James."

"Jolly good," Grandad said. "Hello, James. How are you?"

"Fine, thank you, Mr Hope," James said.

"That's good. Go on in, Gran's in her study typing some letters."

'Gran, I'm here!" Mandy called as she and

James went in through the back door. The click–clack of Gran's old-fashioned typewriter came from the other room. "James is with me."

Mandy looked round the kitchen. There was no sign of the hamster. They went through into Gran's study.

"Hello, you two," Gran said.

Mandy gave her gran a kiss. "Where is he, Gran?"

Gran turned round in her chair and took off her glasses. "If you mean Frisky, I've put him in the spare room. It's nice and light, and warm by the radiator."

"May we go up and see him, please?"

"Of course you can."

Mandy dumped her bag on the floor and ran up the stairs, James close behind. She pushed open the spare bedroom door. On a little table near the radiator was the hamster's cage.

"We mustn't make any loud noises," Mandy whispered. "Hamsters are easily frightened." She bent down to peer into the cage. It was big and had a raised platform

7

with a ladder leading up to it. There was a wheel for Frisky to exercise on and a gnawing block for him to sharpen his teeth. Frisky was inside a wooden box on top of the platform. His little face was peeping out of a nest of soft hay.

Mandy drew in her breath. "Oh, look, James! Isn't he sweet?"

Frisky gazed out at her with jet black, shiny eyes. His nose twitched and his whiskers wiggled.

"He's gorgeous," James said in a hushed voice. "Will he come out, do you think?"

"We might have to wait until it starts to get dark," Mandy said. She knew hamsters usually slept in the daytime.

But as Mandy spoke, Frisky suddenly pushed his way through the hay and popped out on to his platform. He sat up on his hind legs and began washing his face. His paws had four fingers. His little body was round and plump and his fur was brownish-grey.

Mandy was enchanted. She put her finger through the bars of the cage and wiggled it.

"He's very tiny." James peered closer.

"Dad told me he's a Russian hamster," Mandy said. "He said they're much smaller than the golden hamsters that most people have."

"What's that in the corner of the cage?" James pointed to a place where it looked as if Frisky had piled the sawdust up in a heap.

"That must be his food store," Mandy said.

"Food store?" James said, looking puzzled.

"Yes," said Mandy. "Hamsters always

9

make a food store. In the wild they live in the desert so they never know where their next meal's coming from. With a food store they can eat whenever they like."

"I see," said James. "What a good idea."

"You seem to know a lot about it, Mandy." Grandad's voice came from the doorway.

Mandy turned, her eyes shining. "Mum gave me one of those leaflets they keep in the surgery. You know, the ones that tell you all about your pet and how to take care of it properly."

"Oh, yes." Grandad bent down to peer at Frisky. "What do you think of the little fellow, then?"

"He's great," said Mandy and James together. They laughed.

"Can we take him out and play with him?" asked James.

"I think we'd better let him settle down first," Grandad said. "Come and see him again tomorrow. I'm sure he'll be used to his holiday home by then."

There was a bag of hamster mix on the floor beside the table. It was made up of seeds and cereal flakes and dried fruit. There was also a bag of wood shavings for the bottom of Frisky's cage and a bundle of hay for his nest-box.

"Maybe he should have a few more toys," Mandy said to Grandad and James when they had said goodbye to Frisky and were on their way down the stairs. "Hamsters get bored very easily."

"You're the expert," Grandad said. He went to put the kettle on to make a cup of tea.

Gran was still clattering away in her study.

"Tea, Dorothy!" Grandad called. "Want some lemonade, you two?"

"Yes, please," they both said.

Mandy was looking thoughtful. "I'll bring Frisky a tube tomorrow," she said. "You know, one of those from the inside of a kitchen roll."

"What for?" asked James.

"For him to run in and out of," Mandy said. She sat down at the table. "Oh, Grandad, I can't wait to play with him."

Gran came in for her cup of tea.

"Frisky has been asleep since Mary brought him over," she said. "So I haven't had a proper look at him yet."

'Well, he's awake now, Gran, and you can take it from me," Mandy's eyes shone, "he's just gorgeous!"

2

Gran's good idea

When Gran had finished her tea, Mandy and James took her to see Frisky. As they went into the spare bedroom they heard a squeaking noise.

Frisky was fully awake and was inside his exercise wheel, running as fast as he could. The wheel was whizzing round so fast that it was almost a blur. Then Frisky dived out and ran up and down his ladder as fast as he could go.

James and Mandy burst out laughing.

Gran was peering into the cage. "Well, I never," she said, looking amazed.

Frisky stopped dashing round his cage and sat on his hind legs to gnaw a sunflower seed.

"I'll bring him a bit of carrot tomorrow," Mandy said. "And a piece of apple."

"Apple *and* carrot?" Gran laughed.

"Yes," Mandy said. "And celery and lettuce. Hamsters need things like that to keep them healthy."

Gran was still peering at Frisky. "He looks a bit like a mouse to me." She didn't sound sure whether she liked him or not.

"I suppose he does a bit," Mandy said.

"But a nice mouse," James said.

Gran gave a little shiver. "You might think mice are nice, James," she said. "But I don't think I do."

Mandy chuckled. "Well, Frisky's lovely anyway, don't you think?"

Gran still didn't look very sure. "I'll get

used to him, I expect," she said.

"We could help you look after him if you like," Mandy said. "Couldn't we, James?"

"We certainly could," James said.

"That would be lovely," said Gran.

"And Grandad says we can play with him when he's settled down," Mandy said. "We'll come tomorrow if that's OK?"

"Fine with me," Gran said. "I've got a busy week ahead so I'd be grateful if you'd keep Frisky amused."

"We will!" they both said at once.

They said goodbye to Gran and Grandad and made their way home. It was getting dark by now and a grey mist was settling over the village green.

"Bye, James," Mandy said as they parted at James's gate. "I'll call for you in the morning."

Mandy felt happy as she ran off towards Animal Ark. Helping Gran and Grandad look after Frisky would be almost like having a hamster of her own.

A white van with TONY BROWN, PAINTER AND DECORATOR written in big letters on the side stood outside the gate of Animal Ark. The surgery and the house were getting a new coat of paint.

Mandy ran down the brick path and burst in through the door. "Mum! Mum! Where are you?"

"Here, Mandy," Mrs Hope called from the examining room. Mandy ran through.

"Oh, Mum, you must go and see Frisky," she said excitedly. "He's so clever and cute! He's got an exercise wheel and he runs round like mad."

Mrs Hope was hunting for something in a box on the floor. Mr Hope was out on a call.

"I'll pop over as soon as I can," Mrs Hope said. "I'm dying to meet him." She frowned. "Now where is that box of dressings? I can't find a thing since that wretched decorator arrived."

Mandy moved aside another cardboard box and perched herself up on the examining table. She'd had to pack up all her toys and books and take down her animal posters because her bedroom was going to be decorated too. "I wish I could have a hamster of my own," she sighed.

"Sorry, Mandy." Mrs Hope was still rummaging about in the box. "You know the rules. We just haven't got time to look after pets."

"Yes, I know." Mandy brightened up. "Never mind, playing with Frisky during the holiday will be almost as good."

Mrs Hope suddenly gave a shout. "Here it is! I knew it was here somewhere." She took out a box of dressings and put it on top of the cabinet. Then she gave Mandy a quick hug. "I'm sure Gran will be grateful for your help. She's really busy this week organising a jumble sale in the village hall."

"Perhaps James and I could help her with that too?" Mandy said.

"I'm sure you could," Mrs Hope said. "It looks as if you're going to have lots to do this holiday then."

"Yep," Mandy said. "Then there's the firework display. James and I promised to help build the bonfire." She frowned. "I hope people will remember to keep their pets in. They get really scared of fireworks."

There was going to be a huge bonfire and firework display in the field behind the high street. Everyone in the village would be going. James's dad was on the organising committee.

"I'll get Jean to put a reminder on the board in the waiting-room," Mrs Hope said. Jean Knox was Animal Ark's receptionist.

"That's a brilliant idea, Mum," Mandy said.

She got down off the couch and went out to the back room. There were several animals out there. In one wire cage, a large white rabbit with pink eyes was nibbling a carrot.

"What's this bunny here for, Mum?" Mandy called. She opened the cage door and gently stroked the rabbit's fur.

Mrs Hope came through. "He's had a infected foot," she explained. "It's much better now so he's going home tomorrow."

A small black cat was asleep in another cage. Mandy went to look. "What about him?" she asked.

"He's a she," Mrs Hope said with a smile. "She's having an operation tomorrow."

"Poor thing." Mandy gazed at the sleeping cat. She always felt very sad at the thought of animals being ill.

"She's not sick," Mrs Hope explained. "She's just having an operation to prevent her having kittens."

One of the cages was covered with a dark cloth. Mandy lifted a corner and peeped in. A creature about the size of a small rabbit was curled up in a ball in one corner. Mandy drew in her breath.

"What's *that*?"

'A chinchilla," Mrs Hope said.

The chinchilla stirred and stretched. Mandy could see it had thick silver-grey fur, long ears and a bushy tail.

"Isn't he lovely!" Mandy said. She thought the chinchilla was one of the prettiest animals she had ever seen.

"Yes," Mrs Hope said. "They're quite unusual, you know."

"When did he come in, Mum?" asked Mandy.

"Yesterday," Mrs Hope said. "He's not at all well, I'm afraid."

"Oh, dear. What's wrong with him?"

"Some kind of lung infection, we think. He's had some medicine and seems to be getting a bit better."

"I'd love to cuddle him." Mandy looked longingly at the little grey creature.

"Maybe when he's better." Mrs Hope glanced at the clock on the wall. "Come on, Mandy. Dad will be in for his tea soon."

Mandy took one last look at the animals

and followed Mrs Hope through into the house.

It wasn't long before Mr Hope walked in. Mandy told him all about Frisky before he had even had time to take his coat off. He laughed when she told him about the exercise wheel.

"Does it squeak?" he asked.

Mandy grinned. "Yes, it does a bit."

"Put a spot of cooking oil on it," Mr Hope said. "That will cure it and it won't do the hamster any harm if he happens to lick it."

"I'll tell Gran," Mandy said.

They had just finished tea when the phone rang.

"I'll answer it." Mandy ran through into the hall.

"Mandy!" It was Gran and she sounded in a bit of a panic.

"What's up?" Mandy asked.

"It's Frisky," Gran said. "There's something wrong with him. Can you get Mum or Dad to come and take a look at him?"

"Oh, yes, of course," Mandy said. "We'll come straight away." Her stomach turned over. She didn't think she could bear it if Frisky was ill.

She dashed back into the kitchen.

"Mum, Dad," she gasped. "Can you come with me to Gran's? There's something wrong with Frisky."

"Oh dear." Mrs Hope took off her apron. "I'll come. Dad can stay here in case there are any emergency calls. Is that all right, Adam?"

Mr Hope was sitting at the table reading his vet's magazine. "Yes, go ahead. I hope Frisky's all right."

"Oh, so do I," Mandy said.

"We'll take the car," Mrs Hope said when they got outside. "Just in case Frisky needs to come back to the surgery."

Mandy felt sick with worry as she climbed into the car next to her mum. Frisky had been perfectly all right when she and James were at Lilac Cottage earlier on.

They found Gran waiting for them when they arrived. She hurried up the stairs in front of them and thrust open the door to Frisky's room.

"I think he's got mumps," she said anxiously.

Mrs Hope took one look at Frisky and burst out laughing.

"It's not funny, Emily!" Gran sounded indignant. "Look at him!"

Frisky was sitting on top of his nest-box. He gazed at them with beady, bright eyes. His face was huge. His cheeks were puffed out to three times their normal size.

"Oh, Mum!" Mrs Hope laughed and shook her head. "He hasn't got mumps; he's storing food in his cheek pouches!"

"What?" Gran was peering at Frisky with a worried look on her face.

Mrs Hope quickly told Gran that hamsters have large pouches in their cheeks in which to keep food. She pointed to his store in the corner. "They have a food store too, look."

Gran began to laugh too. "Oh, dear," she said, wiping her eyes. "What a silly woman I am." She turned to Mandy. "Honestly, Mandy, I know absolutely nothing about hamsters."

"Never mind, Gran," Mandy said.

"Look," Gran said, "I've got an idea. Why don't you come and stay here for the holidays, Mandy? You could be full time resident hamster-keeper for me." She turned to Mrs Hope. "What do you think, Emily?"

"I think it would be a lovely idea," Mrs Hope said. "It's not much fun at Animal Ark at the moment with ladders and cans of paint all over the place. How about it, Mandy?"

Mandy's eyes were shining. Stay with Gran and look after Frisky for a whole week! It would be fantastic. "Oh, Mum," she said. "Can I really?"

Mrs Hope gave her a hug. "Really," she said. "It will save you popping over here every five minutes."

"Hear that, Frisky?" said Mandy. "I'm going to stay here and look after you."

Frisky gazed at her and twitched his nose.

Mandy looked up at her gran. "He says it's a good idea."

Gran chuckled. "I can see he's going to have the holiday of a lifetime."

"Yes," Mandy said. "And so am I."

3

A spring clean

In the morning Mandy jumped out of bed, dressed quickly and packed a few clothes in her bag. She ran downstairs, ducking under a ladder in the hallway.

Tony Brown was at the top of the ladder painting the ceiling. There were a couple of large paint tins lying open on the floor.

"Morning, Mandy," Tony called as Mandy

sidled past. "Off on your holidays?"

"Yes, I am," Mandy said. She told him where she was going.

"Hamster, eh?" Tony came down the ladder. "Nice things, hamsters. I had one when I was a kid. His name was Lazy."

"Lazy!" Mandy exclaimed. "That's a funny name."

"It wasn't for him," Tony said with a grin. "He slept most of the time."

Mandy laughed. She hoped Frisky wouldn't sleep *all* the time, otherwise she would never get to play with him.

In the kitchen, Mr and Mrs Hope were sitting at the breakfast table.

Mr Hope looked up from his morning paper. "Off to Hamster Hotel then, Mandy?" he said.

"Hamster Hotel!" Mandy laughed. "That's a great name!"

"Frisky's a very lucky little fellow." Mrs Hope got up and put on her white vet's coat. It was almost time for morning surgery. "He'll be the best looked after hamster in Welford, I reckon."

"So do I." Mandy was looking in the bin for the middle of a kitchen roll.

"What are you looking for, Mandy?" her mum asked.

Mandy quickly explained. "Hamsters love running in and out of tunnels," she said.

"There's one in the surgery I think. Come through with me." Mandy followed her mum. "You mustn't give him anything made of soft plastic to play with, you know, Mandy," Mrs Hope said.

"I won't," Mandy said quickly. "He's got very sharp teeth. He'd only bite through it."

"That's right. Plastic wouldn't do his tummy any good at all."

Jean Knox was at her desk opening the day's mail.

"Hello, Jean," Mandy said. "I'm going to be staying at Hamster Hotel for the holiday." She grinned.

"Hamster Hotel?" Jean looked at Mandy over the top of her glasses. "Where on earth's that?"

Mandy told her.

Jean laughed. "Have fun."

★ ★ ★

After breakfast, Mandy washed up, then picked up her bag. "Well, Dad," she said, "I'm off now."

Mr Hope kissed her goodbye. "Me too," he said. "I've got to go up to Syke Farm to look at a sick calf. Have a great time, Mandy." He went through to the surgery to get his bag.

On the way to Lilac Cottage Mandy met Walter Pickard walking to the post office. Walter was an old friend of Mandy's grandad. They were both bell-ringers at the village church.

"Where are you off to then, young miss?" Walter asked when he saw Mandy striding along with her bag. He laughed when she told him she was going to Hamster Hotel.

"And I'd better hurry," she said. "It's time for Frisky's breakfast. Oh, don't forget to keep your cats in on Thursday evening, will you, Mr Pickard?"

Mandy was very fond of Walter's three lively cats, Missie, Tom and Scraps.

Walter frowned. "Thursday evening?"

"Yes," Mandy reminded him. "Bonfire night. There will be lots and lots of fireworks."

"Oh, yes, of course," Walter said. "Thanks for reminding me."

Before she went to Lilac Cottage, Mandy called in at James's to tell him the good news.

"Lucky thing. All those yummy cakes," James said. He was very fond of Gran's baking.

Mandy laughed. "Why don't you come over when you've had breakfast?" she said. "We'll clean Frisky out and have a game with him if he's awake."

"Right." James was trying to stop Blackie from hurtling out of the door. "See you later."

At Lilac Cottage, Gran had just finished typing out a notice announcing the jumble sale.

"Ah, Mandy," she said as Mandy came in and dumped her bag on the chair. "Just the person I wanted to see."

"How's Frisky this morning?" Mandy asked.

"I peeped into his room but he must have been asleep."

Mandy felt disappointed. She would have loved to say hello to Frisky but she knew it would be wrong to disturb him. It looked as if she would have to be up very early in the morning to catch him before he dozed off.

"I'm not surprised he was asleep," Gran said. "I could hear him whizzing round on that wheel all night. He's probably tired out."

Mandy told her about Mr Hope's suggestion to stop the wheel squeaking.

"We can oil it when we clean him out," she said.

"Well," Gran said. "When you've done that will you do something for *me*?"

"Course I will, Gran." Mandy took her bag into the hall. She'd unpack her things later.

Gran was still gazing at the notice she had typed out.

GRAND JUMBLE SALE,
VILLAGE HALL, 2PM SATURDAY
IN AID OF CHURCH FUNDS
If you have any jumble please take it to
Lilac Cottage before Friday.

"Do you think this is all right, Mandy?"
she asked.

"Looks fine to me," Mandy gazed over
Gran's shoulder.

"Right." Gran rolled up the notice.

"Would Jean make some photocopies for me?"

"I'm sure she would," Mandy said.

"And do you think you and James could take them round the village?" Gran asked. "I want as many people to know about the sale as possible."

"OK, Gran," Mandy said. "No problem."

"The vicar might put one on the church notice-board," Gran said thoughtfully.

"Right." Mandy fiddled with her fingers. She was getting impatient to see Frisky. "And I'll ask Jean to put one up at Animal Ark," she said.

"Great," Gran said. "I'm afraid it's a bit short notice. I've been so busy I haven't had time to do them until now." She got up. "Never mind, people usually come up trumps where church funds are concerned."

Mandy was hovering anxiously near the door. "Can I clean Frisky out before I go?"

Gran smiled and gave her a hug. "Of course," she said. "Pets come first!"

Mandy was halfway up the stairs when

there was a knock at the door. She ran back down.

James stood on the doorstep. "I came as quickly as I could," he said. He held up a bag with a carrot and an apple inside. "I've brought Frisky's breakfast."

"Great! Thanks, James. Come on," she said. "We've got a million things to do today."

At first, Frisky was nowhere to be seen. But when Mandy bent to peep into his nest she could just see a hint of grey-brown fur among the soft hay of his bed. There he was, curled up tight as a ball, and fast asleep.

"Is it OK to clean the cage out now?" James asked.

"If we're very careful." Mandy gently unlatched the door of Frisky's cage. "And we shouldn't disturb his food store," she said.

Mandy carefully took out all the old bits of food and wood shavings from the bottom. She put it on some newspaper and wrapped it up. Then she spread out some clean shavings. She put Frisky's toys back in, together with the cardboard roll she had brought from Animal Ark.

Meanwhile, James took Frisky's water bottle and filled it with clean water from the bathroom basin. Frisky's little china food bowl needed filling up, too. James tipped some hamster mix into it then added a piece of apple and carrot.

"Quite a feast," he said.

Mandy smiled. "Hamster Hotel is famous for its good food," she laughed.

Finally, Mandy dabbed a drop of cooking oil on the centre of Frisky's wheel. She spun it round. There wasn't a squeak to be heard.

"There we are," she said when she had finished. "All spick and span."

Frisky had slept through the whole thing. Mandy peered into the nest hopefully. Maybe he would wake up, just for five minutes? But there was no sign of movement. Mandy sighed. They really would have to wait until later to have a game with him.

"Come on," she whispered to James. She picked up the bundle of newspaper. "We'll come back after lunch, shall we? I want to

put some of Gran's posters up round the village."

"Right," James said in a hushed voice.

They tiptoed out of the room and went downstairs.

"What shall I do with this, Gran?" Mandy asked.

Gran eyed the bundle of newspaper. "You can put it on Grandad's compost heap," she said.

"I'll do it." James took the paper from Mandy and went outside. Mandy set off down the path with Gran's jumble sale poster. James soon caught her up and together they made their way towards Animal Ark.

The vicar of Welford, Reverend Hadcroft, was sitting in the waiting-room with a cat basket at his feet. Jean was on the phone.

"Hello, Mr Hadcroft," they said as they came through the door.

"Hello, you two," Mr Hadcroft said.

Mandy sat down beside him. She peered into the basket. "What's wrong with

Jemima? I hope she's not sick."

"No, she's due for an injection, that's all."

Mandy felt relieved. She loved the vicar's tabby cat and would have hated her to be ill.

Mrs Hope's head appeared round the surgery door. "Mr Hadcroft?" she called.

Mr Hadcroft picked Jemima's basket up. "See you, Mandy. See you, James."

Jean Knox was still on the phone. She was talking to Mrs Ponsonby about her Pekinese, Pandora.

"Yes, yes," she was saying. "Mr Hope will come as soon as he can."

"Is Pandora ill?" Mandy asked anxiously when Jean put the phone down.

Jean shook her head. "No, just short of breath," she said. "She needs to go on a diet. That woman spoils her dog rotten."

Mandy showed Jean Gran's poster. "Do you mind if I make some copies?"

"Help yourself," Jean said.

"Thanks," said Mandy, and she and James went through to the back room where the photocopier was kept.

"A dozen should be enough," Mandy said. When they'd finished, she took one through to Jean. "Could you put this up on the board, please, Jean?"

"Will do," Jean said. "Now shoo, you two, I'm very busy."

Mandy and James ran out and made their way down to the post office. Then they worked their way round the village shops. Soon there were posters everywhere.

Mandy hoped Gran's jumble sale would be a great success!

4
Missing!

When Mandy and James got back to Lilac Cottage, Gran was busy sorting out things for the jumble sale. She had filled two black plastic sacks full of old clothes and books. Mandy helped her carry them upstairs.

"About time we got rid of some of this junk," Gran muttered. "Your grandad *will* insist on hoarding things, Mandy.

I'm always telling him off."

Mandy giggled. Grandad *never* threw anything away if he could help it.

"I'm afraid they'll have to go in your room for now, Mandy. There's not really anywhere else to put them." Gran dumped the bags by the cupboard door. "Someone will come round on Friday to pick them up."

Mandy peered hopefully into Frisky's cage. But he was still asleep. The cage was as neat as a new pin. Mandy tried not to be disappointed. She would just have to be patient. There would be plenty of time to play with Frisky that evening.

And when she and James went upstairs after tea there was Frisky, sitting at the bottom of his ladder nibbling a piece of apple.

Mandy drew in her breath. "Isn't he wonderful?" She put her finger through the bars and waggled it. Frisky finished his apple and scampered over to his food bowl. Soon he was gobbling up his hamster mix. Most of it went into his cheek pouches.

"He looks as if he's got mumps again,"

James laughed. He had heard all about Gran's mistake. "Why don't we take him down to show your gran and grandad?"

Gran was getting ready to go out. There was a meeting of the jumble sale committee and Gran was chairman.

She peered into the cage. "Oh, yes." She still didn't sound too sure. "He is rather sweet after all."

Mandy put the cage on the coffee table in the living-room where Grandad was watching his favourite gardening programme.

Frisky had finished his tea and was running in and out of the cardboard tube.

Grandad peered into the cage. "What a cute little fellow," he said. "Shall we let him out to have a run round?"

Mandy's eyes lit up. It was just what she and James had been waiting for.

"Oh, Grandad, can we?" she said.

Grandad cocked his head to one side. "I think we'd better wait until your Gran's gone, though, don't you? She might not like him running round the living-room."

Gran poked her head round the door.

"I'm just off, Tom," she said.

"OK," Grandad waved his hand. "See you later."

They waited until they heard the door bang shut.

"Right," Grandad said. "Coast's clear. Let's make sure there are no holes for him to disappear down first."

James and Mandy searched the room thoroughly.

"No holes!" they said.

"And all the windows are shut," Mandy added.

"I'll put the guard round the hearth." Grandad got up and put the big brass fender in front of the fire. "There, that should be OK."

Mandy was so excited, her heart was beating like a drum as she opened the cage door. She put her hand slowly inside. She picked the hamster up gently and lifted him out.

Frisky sat on the palm of her hand looking at her. "I think he likes me," Mandy said.

"Sensible chap," Grandad chuckled.

Suddenly Frisky turned and ran up Mandy's arm. He sat on her shoulder, then disappeared inside the collar of her sweat-shirt. She sat perfectly still. She could feel Frisky running down her back and round her waist. It tickled so much it was all she could do to stop herself wriggling. Then, suddenly, he appeared on her lap.

"Could I hold him?" James had been watching.

"Of course you can."

Mandy picked Frisky up and passed him to James. He stroked the hamster then put him on his knee. Frisky suddenly ran round James's waist and disappeared.

James sat as still as a stone. "Where's he gone?" He hardly dared breathe.

"I don't know," Mandy said.

Then a lump appeared in the pocket of James's tracksuit top.

Grandad roared with laughter. "He's in your pocket," he said. "The cheeky little blighter."

Suddenly Frisky's nose appeared and he scampered out of James's pocket, down the

side of the chair and on to the floor. He ran around, then disappeared under the sideboard.

Mandy lay flat on the floor. She could see Frisky sitting on his hind legs by the skirting-board. He was gazing back at her with bright, beady eyes.

Suddenly the door opened and Gran came in.

"Forgot my notebook," she said, heading for her study.

"Gran!" Mandy gasped. "Shut the . . ."

But it was too late, Frisky had spotted the opening. He dropped down on all fours and scurried out of the room as fast as he could.

"Oh, no," Mandy wailed. "He's gone out!" She dashed into the hall.

Gran looked round. "Who has?"

"Frisky," James said. He ran out after Mandy.

Grandad sat in his chair, chuckling. "He won't go far, Mandy," he called. "Don't worry." Then he suddenly looked serious. "I hope you shut the back door, Dorothy."

"Yes, I did," she said.

"Thank goodness for that," Grandad said.

By now Frisky had completely disappeared. Mandy and James ran all over looking for him.

"Do you think he could have got up the stairs?" James asked.

Mandy shook her head. She felt close to tears. "I don't know," she wailed.

Gran came back out with her notebook. She was walking very carefully, afraid she might step on the escaped hamster.

"You'll have to find him, Mandy." Gran

looked serious. "Mary won't be very pleased if she comes back from holiday and he's gone missing."

"I know, Gran. I'm really sorry," Mandy said, close to tears.

Gran put her arm round her. "It was my fault for opening that door."

Mandy shook her head. "No, it wasn't. I shouldn't have let him out. I just wanted to hold him." A tear ran down her cheek.

Gran gave her a quick hug. "Don't worry, Mandy, he's got to be in the house somewhere. If he's still missing I'll help look when I get back." She slipped out of the back door, shutting it quickly behind her.

Mandy and James searched for Frisky until it was time for James to go home.

Mandy's face was glum as she said goodbye to him at the front door.

"I just don't know what we're going to do," she said. She couldn't bear to think of the little creature lost somewhere.

"You could make a trap," James suggested.

Mandy looked at him in horror. "What? Like a mouse-trap?"

"No, silly," James said. "A bottle."

Mandy looked puzzled. "What do you mean?"

"Well," James said. "You get a tall glass jar and put some food and bedding in it."

"Then what?" Mandy asked.

"Then you leave it sideways on the floor. When the hamster goes in to get the food he can't climb out through the neck, it's too slippery."

Mandy's face brightened. "How do you know all this?"

"I read it in a book," James said. He zipped up his coat. "It's supposed to work every time."

"James, you're brilliant!" Mandy cried.

"I know." James laughed as he let himself out through the front door.

Mandy closed the door behind him and sighed. She hoped James was right about the hamster trap. If not, she didn't know *what* they were going to do.

"Any sign of the little chap?" Grandad asked when Mandy got back into the front room.

She shook her head. "No." She went on to tell Grandad about James's idea.

"Right." Grandad turned off the television. "One of those tall jars Gran uses for bottling fruit would be ideal, I reckon. There's a whole shelf of them in the pantry." While Grandad got one down Mandy went upstairs and got some hamster mix and bedding. She took a piece of carrot and apple. If they didn't tempt Frisky then nothing would.

"We'll put it in the living-room," Grandad said. "Let's hope he finds it."

That night Mandy lay awake. She kept imagining all sorts of things that might have happened to Frisky. What if he was stuck somewhere? Maybe he was hiding in a cupboard? She had hunted again before she went to bed but there was no trace of him anywhere.

In the middle of the night Mandy awoke from a restless doze. The moon was shining brightly through the gap in her curtains. Mandy got out of bed and crept downstairs. It was no good. She *had* to see if Frisky was in the jar.

Mandy tiptoed into the living-room. Gran had drawn back the curtains and the room was bright with moonlight. The jar lay near the fender where Mandy had left it. She let out a sigh of disappointment.

The jar was empty!

5

Never a dull moment

Mandy felt close to tears. Then she suddenly realised the apple and the carrot were gone from the jar. The little bundle of hay began to twitch and all of a sudden out popped Frisky. He ran towards the neck of the jar but kept slipping and sliding backwards. James had been right. Frisky couldn't escape.

"Frisky!" Mandy almost shouted for joy. "Thank goodness!" She scooped up the jar and carried it up to her bedroom. "You naughty boy," she scolded as she climbed the stairs. "Don't you ever frighten me like that again!"

As she went along the landing Gran's bedroom door opened. Gran appeared, looking sleepy-eyed.

"Are you all right, Mandy? I heard you go downstairs."

"Yes, thanks, Gran. I'm fine." She held up the jar. "Look!"

"Well, thank goodness for that," Gran said with a sigh. "Is he all right?"

"He's fine," Mandy said.

"Now perhaps we can get some sleep," Gran said. "Grandad's been tossing and turning ever since we got to bed. Who would have thought such a little creature would cause so much worry?" She waggled her finger at Frisky. "Now you behave yourself, young fellow!" She winked at Mandy then went back into her room and closed the door.

Mandy took Frisky into her room. She gently shook him out of the jar and popped him back into his cage. Frisky ran to his exercise wheel, hopped in and began running. The wheel whizzed round and round. He seemed none the worse for his adventure.

Mandy climbed back into bed and was asleep almost as soon as her head touched the pillow.

Next morning she phoned James to tell him the good news.

"Can I bring Blackie round?" James said when she had told him the story. "We said we'd do some training with him, remember?"

"OK," Mandy said. She smiled to herself. Training Blackie was always great fun, although very rarely successful!

Grandad was just going out to do some work in the garden. He was in a strange mood that morning. Mandy had heard him opening and closing drawers and muttering to himself. Then he had stomped downstairs, grabbed a coat from the hall cupboard and gone out, still mumbling something under his breath.

"Could you take that barrowload of cuttings round to the bonfire later, please, Mandy?" he asked as she stepped outside to see if James and Blackie were coming. "They're quite dry and should burn jolly well."

Just then James and Blackie appeared round the side of the cottage. Blackie had his ball in his mouth. He barged through the gate, almost pulling James over.

"Dad's got some old timber for the bonfire," James panted. "I promised him we'd cart that over too. We'll do some training with Blackie first though, shall we, Mandy?"

"If you like," Mandy said.

Grandad grinned. He had seen them trying to train Blackie before. "Good luck," he said and disappeared into his garden shed.

Gran was just going off to her exercise class. Mandy went with her to the front gate.

"If anyone brings any jumble don't forget it's got to go upstairs," Gran reminded her. "I don't want it cluttering up the hall and front room."

"I won't," Mandy promised. "See you later, Gran." She waved as Gran headed off in the direction of the village hall. Then she turned to James. "What are we going to do with Blackie today?" she asked.

"Retrieving," James said. He tried to get the ball out of Blackie's mouth. Blackie growled playfully and twisted his head from side to side. "Labradors are good at that."

"Leave!" Mandy shook her finger at Blackie.

Blackie stared at her from under his eyelids.

"Leave!" she said again.

"Here, Blackie." James took a dog-biscuit from his pocket. Blackie dropped the ball and gobbled up the biscuit. Mandy dived for it.

"Right," she said. "Here we go."

Mandy and James spent the whole morning trying to get Blackie to bring the

ball back. No matter how hard they tried, Blackie would insist on running off round and round the garden with it.

Grandad thought it was better than a comedy show. "You'll have to put him on a long lead and *make* him bring it back," he called, laughing. He leaned on his spade, watching Blackie running round with Mandy and James chasing him.

"It's no good," James panted. "I give in. Blackie's no good at bringing things back and that's that."

Just then a sleek saloon car pulled up out–side. A large lady got out. She was wearing a tweed suit and a black hat. It was Mrs Ponsonby. Pandora the Pekinese was peeping out of the window from her special compartment in the back.

"Mr Hope!" Mrs Ponsonby was round the back of the car in three long strides. "I've brought some things for the sale."

"Oh, good morning, Mrs Ponsonby," Grandad called. He put down his spade and hurried to the gate. "That's very kind of you, thank you very much."

"There's one of darling Pandora's old baskets." Mrs Ponsonby opened the boot. "And some other bits and pieces." She piled the basket and several cardboard boxes into Grandad's arms.

James and Mandy ran to help when they saw Grandad was having a problem balancing all the boxes in his arms. Mandy said hello to Pandora as she passed, then ran to take a box.

Blackie, meanwhile, lay on the grass, the ball clamped firmly between his jaws.

"How's Pandora, Mrs Ponsonby?" Mandy asked.

"She's been a bit poorly," Mrs Ponsonby replied. "But I've kept her in bed for a couple of days and she seems a bit better, aren't you, darling?" she cooed to Pandora.

Mandy peered through the window. "Maybe a long walk would do her good?" she suggested. "Most dogs love walks."

Mrs Ponsonby shook her head. "It would only tire her out, poor lamb," she said.

Pandora was looking at Mandy with her black, boot-button eyes. She gave a yap then yawned. She lay down, sighed and closed her eyes. Mandy smiled. Pandora obviously didn't think much of *that* idea. "Don't forget to keep her in on Thursday evening, will you?" she said.

"Thursday evening?" Mrs Ponsonby looked puzzled.

"The bonfire," Mandy said.

"Oh, yes, of course!" Mrs Ponsonby exclaimed. "Those horrible fireworks. Don't worry, I'll make sure Pandora is tucked up safely in bed."

Mandy smiled again. Pandora certainly was the most spoiled dog around.

She helped Grandad take the stuff upstairs.

"Someone else is here with some jumble," James called as they went back out into the garden.

"Phew." Grandad took off his cap and wiped his brow. "*When* am I going to get my gardening done?"

By the time Thursday came there was a great pile of jumble in Mandy's room. In fact there was so much that it had spilled out on to the landing. Boxes of books and bric-a-brac, old toys, clothes and all kinds of other things.

"Gran will be pleased," Mandy said as she helped Grandad cart yet another load up the stairs.

"She certainly will," Grandad said. "Everyone's gone mad, I reckon. Some of this stuff is as good as new."

Mandy smiled to herself. She thought of Grandad's favourite old gardening jumper. He always said *that* was as good as new even though it was full of holes. Gran was always telling him he should throw it away.

Every day Mandy and James made sure Frisky's cage was spick and span and he had plenty of fresh food and water.

Frisky usually woke up about teatime. His antics kept Mandy and James in fits. There was certainly never a dull moment when Frisky was awake. And they were very careful never to let him escape again.

By now, the bonfire in the field behind the village high street looked like a mountain. When they weren't looking after Frisky or taking Blackie for walks, Mandy and James helped to build it.

"I hope they're going to make sure no hedgehogs have crawled under it," Mandy said to James as they tipped yet another barrowload of Grandad's garden cuttings on to the heap.

"Dad built a platform first," James assured her. "That means they should be able to see if there are any underneath before they light it."

"Brilliant," Mandy said. She grabbed the empty barrow and ran on ahead. "I can't wait for tonight."

The bonfire was to be lit at six o'clock. Mandy made sure Frisky had enough food and water for the evening then put on her coat and boots.

Outside it was a chilly, misty evening. People were already making their way along the high street towards the field where the bonfire stood.

Mandy walked between Gran and Grandad. Her mum and dad were waiting for them outside Animal Ark. They were meeting James and Mrs Hunter at the bonfire. Mr Hunter had gone earlier to make sure the firework display was ready.

"While I think of it, Mandy," her mum said as they strolled past the post office and down the narrow alley that led to the bonfire field, "would you like to come shopping in Walton tomorrow?"

"That would be great," Mandy said. "I bet James would like to come too. I'll ask him." Her eyes lit up as she suddenly had an idea. "I could get Frisky a present to remind him of his holiday at Hamster Hotel!"

Mrs Hope smiled. "How's he getting on?"

"He's fine," Mandy said. She tried not to think about how much she would miss Frisky when Mary came to collect him.

A large crowd had gathered round the bonfire. Almost everyone in the village had turned up.

Mandy ran off to find James. He was standing behind the ropes watching his dad getting ready to light the huge bonfire.

There was a stall nearby selling hot dogs and hot baked potatoes and the smell made Mandy's stomach rumble.

She asked James if he would like to go shopping the following day. "I'm going to get Frisky a present," she told him.

"That sounds great!" James jumped up and down to try to keep warm. "Maybe we could buy a really good one between us?"

"Let's go and see your dad." Mandy scrambled under the rope and ran over to Mr Hunter. James followed.

"Have you checked for hedgehogs?" Mandy asked anxiously.

Mr Hunter nodded. "There weren't any," he said. "Now get back behind the ropes, please, you two," he added. "It's not safe here."

When Mandy and James rejoined the crowd, Mr Hunter lit the taper and there was a shout as the bonfire caught and roared. The orange flames lit up the night sky. Everyone clapped.

Then, with a bang and a shower of sparks, the firework display began.

Even though she was enjoying herself, Mandy couldn't help worrying about the village pets.

"I do hope everyone remembered to keep their dogs and cats in," she said in James's ear after a very loud bang that echoed around the field like thunder.

"Well, Blackie and Benji are tucked up safe and sound," James said.

Mandy suddenly decided she couldn't resist the smell of the hot dogs any longer.

"Do you want a hot dog, James?"

"Mmm," James licked his lips. "Yes, please."

They wandered over to the stall where Mr Oliver was dishing out the food.

Mandy had just finished eating when she spotted a dark shadow by the hedge. She clutched James's arm.

"James, look! What's that over there?"

James peered into the shadows. "Where?"

Mandy pointed. She couldn't believe her eyes. A small black dog was creeping along the edge of the field.

"There!" she cried. "Come on, James, quick!" Mandy ran across, James right behind her.

By now, the little creature was crouched by the gatepost, hunched up, its tail between its legs. It was trembling with fright. It flinched as a rocket took off and exploded in a blizzard of stars.

Just as it was about to dash off into the road, Mandy grabbed it. The dog was freezing cold and whimpering with fear. Mandy crouched down and scooped him up into her arms. She noticed he was wearing a collar with a silver disc attached to it.

"Oh, James, he's terrified." She stroked the dog's head. How could anyone be so cruel as to let their dog out on a night like this?

"Poor thing," Mandy was murmuring. "Come on, James, let's get him away from the noise."

Cradling the dog against her coat Mandy strode through the gate.

"Where are you taking him?" James hurried after her.

"Back to Animal Ark," she said. "He'll be safe there."

Gran and Grandad were talking to Walter Pickard. Mandy waited while James ran to tell them where they were going. Then they headed off across the village green towards Animal Ark. The dog was trembling and making little whining noises.

"Don't worry," Mandy soothed. "You're safe now." She unzipped her jacket and put it round him. The sooner they got the little dog into the warmth of Animal Ark, the better.

6

A present for Frisky

Indoors, Mandy got a blanket and wrapped it round the little dog. She sat by the fire, hugging him on her lap. James bent down to stroke his head. The dog had stopped shaking and had nestled as close to Mandy as he could.

"Here," Mandy said to James. "You hold him while I heat up some milk. It'll warm his

tummy up and make him feel much better."

A few minutes later Mandy poured the milk carefully into a small bowl. James put the dog down on the floor. He wobbled a bit then sniffed the milk. Soon he began to lap it up. Mandy kneeled beside him.

"I wonder why his owners didn't shut him in," she said. "They should have known how scared he'd be."

"Have a look on his collar," James said. "It should tell us where he lives."

Mandy turned over the silver disc. "His

name's Bobby," she said. "And there's just a phone number. Welford 876597." She stood up. "I'd better give them a ring. They'll probably be worried about him."

Just then the door opened and Mr Hope came hurrying in. He had come as soon as he heard what had happened. "Gran told me you were here." He bent down. "Is he all right?"

The little dog had finished the milk. He sat huddled up close to the fire. He was licking his chops and looking at Mr Hope with wide, scared eyes.

Mr Hope held his head and looked into his eyes. He ran his hand down his back and legs. "He seems OK now."

Mandy gave the little mongrel a hug. "His name's Bobby," Mandy said. "I was just going to ring his owners."

She went out into the hall to use the phone. A minute or two later, she came back. "He comes from those houses behind the church," she said. "I said we'd take him home."

"Did they know he was out?" James asked.

"Yes. They were really worried. He

belongs to their little girl and she's been crying all evening. They said they had been looking everywhere for him. He's always running away."

"Well, this might have taught him a lesson," Mr Hope said. "Although it's really up to the owners to keep their dogs under control."

Mr Hope went to get a spare dog lead he kept in the surgery. When he came back Mandy and James were ready to go.

"Gran and Grandad have gone home," Mr Hope told her. "I'll give them a ring to tell them you're on your way back."

"Thanks," Mandy said.

"We missed the rest of the fireworks," James remarked as they hurried along the main street towards the church.

"Never mind," Mandy said. "I would rather have been helping Bobby."

"Me too," James agreed.

They found Bobby's house and knocked at the door. A little girl answered it. Her eyes were red and she looked very unhappy. Her face lit up though, when she saw Mandy and James standing on the doorstep with Bobby.

When he saw her, Bobby's tail began wagging nineteen to the dozen. He gave a little whine and began jumping up at her.

The little girl burst into tears and bent down to pick him up.

"Oh, Bobby, you naughty boy!" she sobbed, burying her face in the soft fur of his neck.

Bobby began whining and licking her face.

"Oh, Bobby," she said again.

Mandy felt like crying too. Bobby's owner had obviously been frantic.

"My dad says he's all right," Mandy said. "But he's had a very lucky escape," she added gently. "You'll have to keep a close eye on him from now on."

"We will, I promise." The girl wiped her eyes. "Thank you very much."

They could hear her still talking to Bobby as she turned back into the house and closed the door.

When Mandy had said goodbye to James and got back to Lilac Cottage, Gran had a steaming cup of hot chocolate ready for her.

"How did you get on?" she asked as

Mandy came in. "Poor little dog."

"OK," Mandy said. She told her gran about the little girl.

"I bet you told her off," Grandad said when he came in. He knew how angry Mandy got if she thought animals were not being looked after properly.

"No, I didn't," Mandy said. "She was too upset."

Grandad gave Mandy a hug. "Bobby was a very lucky dog if you ask me," he said.

Mandy finished her drink and ran upstairs to see Frisky. He was dashing round and round the cage, up his ladder, through his cardboard tunnel and in and out of his exercise wheel. The wheel was squeaking badly again. Cooking oil didn't seem to last very long.

Mandy decided Frisky was quite the most charming pet she had ever *almost* had, even though she sometimes felt quite tired just watching him!

She sat by his cage and told Frisky about the night's adventures. He seemed to listen to every word she was saying. Then she took him out and let him have a little run around. She picked him up and he sat on her hand. Then he darted up her sleeve, sat on her collar for a moment and disappeared down her neck.

Mandy chuckled. She was quite used to the feeling of Frisky running about inside her clothes by now. When he popped out of her sleeve again she caught him and put him carefully back into his cage.

She sighed. She was really going to miss Frisky when it was time for him to go home.

The following morning Mrs Hope picked up Mandy and James to take them shopping. Before they set off, she paid a visit to Frisky. He was very sleepy and almost ready for his daytime snooze.

"He's really sweet," Mrs Hope said. "And very clean and healthy. You're doing a grand job, you two."

On the way to Walton, Mandy gazed out of the window at the passing fields and trees. The mist of the early morning had given way to bright sunshine. Tomorrow she would be busy helping with the jumble sale and the next day Frisky would be going home and she would be going back to Animal Ark. The week seemed to have flashed by.

"What are we going to get Frisky?" James asked.

Mandy was thoughtful. "I'm not sure. We'll have to look and see what they've got in the pet shop."

"He's already got a wheel, a tube and a gnawing block," James said.

Mrs Hope laughed. "Well, what *do* you buy the hamster who's got everything?"

"A friend?" James suggested.

Mandy shook her head. "No, hamsters have to live on their own. They fight if you put two together."

Mrs Hope came up with an idea. "You could make him an adventure playground," she suggested.

"Adventure playground?" Mandy said.

"Yes, you could put a small branch into the cage and put little ladders up one side and down the other. Grandad would find you something suitable and you could get the ladders in Walton."

"What a great idea, Mum! We could make it when we get back."

There was a pet shop in Walton where they found just the ladders they wanted. They were made of metal and had hooks at the end.

"We can hook them over the branch," Mandy said. "He's going to love it, I know."

"Then we could hang something to one end of the branch," James suggested.

"What sort of thing?" Mandy asked.

"How about a couple of wooden cotton reels?" Mrs Hope suggested. "They make great hamster toys."

Mandy and James bought one ladder each. Then they bought a new gnawing block as Frisky had almost bitten his way through his old one. It was important for hamsters to keep their teeth short. Last of all, they bought a bag of special luxury hamster mix.

On the way home, they sat in the back of the car making plans.

"We can set the adventure playground up in Frisky's cage while he's asleep," said Mandy.

"Then it will be a surprise when he wakes

up," James said excitedly. "I just can't wait to see what he does!"

"Neither can I," Mandy chuckled.

When they got back to Lilac Cottage, Grandad was outside cleaning the windows. Mandy told him about Frisky's surprise and asked if he would help them.

"Oh, I should think so." Grandad put down his polishing cloth. "Follow me."

He strode off down the path. "I've had a really busy morning," he told them as they went down to the bottom of the garden. "First the car wouldn't start when Gran wanted to go shopping. Then just as I got *that* sorted, John Jenkins came to pick up the jumble. Ah . . ."

He stopped under one of the apple-trees that grew by the fence. "An apple twig," he said. He took out his penknife and cut one off. "Just the job for a hamster's adventure playground. What do you think?"

Mandy took it from him. "Great. Thanks, Grandad."

She suddenly thought of something else. "Do you think Gran would mind if we looked in her sewing box?"

"What for?" Grandad asked.

"A couple of empty wooden cotton reels," James said. "We're going to hang them from the branch."

"I'm sure she won't mind," Grandad said. "Make sure you put everything back, though."

"We will." Mandy and James dashed indoors.

Mandy found two suitable cotton reels while James found some string in a kitchen drawer. Together they tied them on to the apple twig.

Mandy sat back. "Frisky's going to have great fun with those," she said. "Come on, let's set it up while he's still asleep."

They took everything upstairs. Mandy put her finger to her lips. "Let's be very quiet," she whispered.

She opened the door softly. Then she froze with shock. The table by the radiator was empty. It wasn't only the stuff for the jumble sale that had gone.

Frisky had gone too!

7

All locked up

Mandy and James stood gazing at the empty table. They could hardly believe Frisky had just vanished into thin air.

Then Mandy gave a little laugh of relief. "Gran must have moved him," she said. "She knew Mr Jenkins was coming this morning. Maybe she's put Frisky in the living-room."

They ran downstairs. Frisky *wasn't* in the living-room. They looked in the study, then over the rest of the house. Frisky was nowhere to be found.

"Let's go and ask your grandad," James said.

They dashed outside.

"Grandad, where's Frisky?" she called anxiously.

"Frisky? In your room, isn't he?" Grandad had finished cleaning the windows and was in his potting shed.

Mandy shook her head. "No, he's gone."

Grandad tipped his cap to the back of his head and frowned. "Come on, let's have a look."

Mandy and James followed him indoors and back upstairs. "He's not there, honestly," Mandy wailed.

"We've looked *everywhere*," James added.

Grandad stood in the bedroom doorway, his hands on his hips. "Well, I don't know, I'm sure . . ."

Mandy was beginning to feel desperate. Where *could* Frisky have gone?

Then James had an idea.

"Maybe he went with the jumble," he said.

Mandy looked at him in horror. "Surely no one would think we were giving Frisky to a jumble sale," she said.

James shrugged. "If he was asleep in his nest Mr Jenkins wouldn't have been able to see him, would he?"

Grandad looked thoughtful. "You know, James is right," he said. "John might have thought it was an empty cage."

"Oh, Grandad!" Mandy could hardly hold back the tears.

"Come on," Grandad said. He put his arm round her. "Let's give John a ring."

They went back down the stairs. Grandad dialled Mr Jenkins's number but there was no reply.

"Can't we go to his house?" Mandy asked anxiously. "He might just be out in the garden and not able to hear the phone."

Grandad shook his head. "I'm sorry, Mandy, I don't know where he lives. We'll have to wait until your gran gets back from the supermarket. She'll know."

"He wouldn't have taken the jumble to his house though, would he?" James piped up.

Mandy stared at him. Then her face cleared. "No, of *course* he wouldn't!" she said. "He would have taken it to the village hall. Let's go and see." She rushed off to get her coat.

"But it'll be all locked up," Grandad called as they ran out. "You should wait till Gran gets back."

"We'll go and see anyway," Mandy shouted, halfway down the path. "It won't do any harm."

She couldn't possibly wait until Gran got back. She might be ages. She had to do something *now*.

Mandy and James raced down the high street across the green to the village hall. Jean Knox was just coming out of the post office.

"What's the rush, Mandy?" she called.

Mandy skidded to a halt and quickly told Jean what had happened.

"Oh, dear," Jean said. "I hope you find him all right. Let me know if I can help."

"We will!" James called as they rushed off.

Mr Hadcroft was pinning a notice on the church notice-board. Mandy was in such a hurry she nearly ran into him.

"Hey, hey . . . !" He took hold of her arms. "Where's the fire?"

"We've lost Frisky," Mandy panted. She went on to tell him the story.

Mr Hadcroft patted her shoulder. "Well, try not to worry, Mandy, I'm sure he'll be OK."

"I do hope so." Mandy still felt close to tears.

"If I see John Jenkins, I'll tell him," Mr Hadcroft called.

"Thanks," Mandy shouted over her shoulder.

They reached the village hall and hurried through the gate and up the steps. Mandy grabbed the door handle. She twisted and pushed. Nothing happened. Grandad had been right. The hall was all locked up.

James jumped up and down, trying to see

through one of the windows. "I can't reach," he panted.

"Here," Mandy tried to lift him up but he kept slipping out of her grasp.

"It's no good," she panted. "You're too heavy. Can't we find something to stand on?" She looked round desperately.

There was an orange plastic milk crate by the back door. Mandy went to fetch it. She turned it upside down and stood on it.

"I still can't see," she wailed. She was standing on tiptoe and the crate was wobbling like mad.

"You'll fall off," James warned.

Mandy got down. She sat on the crate and put her head in her hands. "Oh, James; poor Frisky. What are we going to do?"

James sat beside her. "Maybe we should go back home and wait for your gran."

"I'm not budging until I find out if he's in there!" Mandy said stubbornly.

James sighed. "OK, but I don't know what good it will do."

Luckily it wasn't long before they spotted Gran's car coming along the road.

Mandy jumped to her feet. "Gran!" She ran to the kerb and waved her arms. "Gran! Gran! Stop!"

Gran pulled up beside her. She wound down the window. "Mandy, what's wrong?" she asked anxiously.

Mandy's words all seemed to tumble over one another as she told Gran what had happened.

"Oh dear." Gran gave a little chuckle. "Poor Frisky. Hop in, you two, I'll take you to John Jenkins's house. He's bound to have a key." When she saw Mandy's worried face she stopped smiling. "Don't worry, Mandy, I'm sure Frisky will be all right."

"That's what everyone keeps saying," Mandy wailed. "But it will be cold and draughty in the hall and he'll be scared stiff if he wakes up in a strange place."

Gran patted her knee. "We'll soon sort this out, don't worry. And he'll be quite safe in his cage, you know."

When they reached Mr Jenkins's house Gran knocked at the door but there was still no answer and the windows were all in darkness.

Mandy jiggled about in her seat. "Oh, James," she said. "What on earth are we going to do now?"

8

Safe and sound

Gran came back to the car looking thoughtful. She got in and started the engine.

"We'll have to go and get the key from Mr Markham," she said.

"Who's he?" James asked as they drove back towards the village centre.

"Chairman of the parish council," Gran told them. "I know he's got a key to the hall. I have to collect it from him before our WI meetings."

"I hope *he's* in,' Mandy said. "Otherwise I don't know what we're going to do."

They drew up outside Number 2, The Terrace, the home of Mr Markham.

"You two stay here in the warm," Gran said. "I'll go and see."

Mandy peered out of the car window anxiously. It was getting dark now and a cold wind was blowing. There wouldn't be any heating in the village hall. She felt sick with fear. If Frisky was in there it would be much too cold for him.

It wasn't long before someone answered the door. Gran disappeared inside for a minute or two then came back out waving a key. She hurried down the path and got into the car.

"Here we are," she said briskly. She gave the key to Mandy. "Problem solved."

Gran drove quickly along the main street to the village hall. She pulled up outside and Mandy and James jumped out. Mandy unlocked the door and ran inside.

Quickly she clicked on the light. The jumble *was* here. Piles of it. Bags, boxes, even suitcases full of old clothes, all waiting to be sorted out the following morning. Someone had already put up long trestle-tables.

Mandy gave a shiver. It felt freezing, just as she had feared it would be. Frisky would be cold and frightened and so bewildered he wouldn't know *where* he was.

But where *was* Frisky? Mandy and James carefully pulled aside bags and boxes but there wasn't a hamster cage of any description anywhere.

Mandy sat on a chair and burst into tears.

"Don't cry, Mandy," James said. "He's got to be somewhere."

Gran joined them and put her arm round Mandy.

"Don't upset yourself, darling. John must have spotted him and taken him home," Gran said.

"But John's not *at* home," Mandy sobbed.

Gran got up. "We'll return Mr Markham's key, then we'll go and see if John's back."

But when they reached Mr Jenkins's house, it was still in total darkness.

"I'll pop next door," Gran said. "They might know how long he'll be."

When she came back she shook her head. "Sorry, Mandy, he won't be back until late. I'm afraid we'll just have to wait until the morning."

They dropped James off at his gate.

"I'll come round early and see what's happened," he said.

"OK." Mandy sat sadly in the back of the car. She didn't know *how* she was going to get any sleep that night. She would be worrying about Frisky all the time.

When they got home, Grandad was waiting anxiously.

"Any luck?" he asked as they came in.

Gran shook her head. "No, I'm afraid not."

Grandad put his arm round Mandy. "Try not to worry, love," he said. "He's got a snug nest and plenty of food. He'll be all right."

It seemed really quiet in Mandy's room with no hamster whizzing round on his wheel or tearing in and out of his cardboard roll. His adventure playground still lay on the table where Mandy and James had left it.

About ten o'clock Mandy heard the phone ring and Gran's voice answering it. Then Gran came up the stairs. The bedroom door opened.

"Are you asleep, Mandy?"

"No, Gran," she said. "What's up?"

"John Jenkins has just phoned," Gran told her.

Mandy sat up quickly. Her heart thudded. "What did he say?" she asked anxiously.

Gran sat on the bed. "It seems the whole village has found out about Frisky," she said with a smile. "Jean saw Walter in the Fox and Goose. Walter told Mr Hadcroft who said he knew already. Mr Hadcroft phoned Mr Markham who had just got home. Mr Markham phoned John and John phoned me." Gran chuckled. "Quite a jungle telegraph."

Mandy wrung her hands together. "But, Gran, what about *Frisky*?"

"John's got him at home," Gran said with

a smile. "He's absolutely fine."

"Oh, thank goodness!" Mandy threw her arms round her gran's neck in delight.

Gran laughed. "Hey, you're strangling me."

Mandy let go. "Sorry, Gran." Her eyes were shining. "Tell me what happened."

"Wait and see John in the morning," Gran said. "He's taking Frisky to the hall first thing. I said you and James would go and help them sort out the jumble. John can tell you the story himself then."

9

None the worse

The next morning James turned up bright
and early. Mandy was still having breakfast.

"Sit down and have some toast and
home-made jam," Gran said to James when
he arrived. "I'll make you a hot chocolate."

"Thanks, Mrs Hope." James sat down
next to Mandy. "Have you had any news
about Frisky?" he asked anxiously. "I've

been thinking about him all night."

Mandy quickly told him about John's late-night phone call.

"Thank goodness!" James heaped a spoonful of strawberry jam on to his toast. "I hardly slept a wink."

"Are you coming to help sort out the jumble, Tom?" Gran asked Grandad.

Grandad looked up from his gardening magazine. "If you want me to, Dorothy."

"The more the merrier." Gran began clearing away the dishes. Mandy got up to give her a hand but she was in such a hurry she almost dropped a plate. Gran took it from her.

"I can see you're dying to get down to that hall, love," she said. "Off you go, both of you. We'll come along a bit later."

James snatched up the last of his toast and they set off.

"You've got jam all round your mouth." Mandy grinned at James as they hurried along to the hall. She felt on top of the world now she knew Frisky was safe and sound. She just couldn't wait to see him again.

James licked round his mouth. He screwed up his nose and looked at Mandy. "Has it gone?"

"Yep." Mandy grinned. "Race you!" They took off down the street, shouting noisily.

When they got there, the hall was a hive of activity. Half a dozen ladies were sorting out old clothes, a teenage girl was in charge of the tapes and CDs and Mr Hadcroft was arranging a pile of toys.

There was a woman folding up pairs of trousers and putting them in a pile on the table by the door.

"Can we see Mr Jenkins, please?" Mandy panted. She had arrived just seconds before James.

"He's over by the stage." The woman pointed. "Sorting out the garden tools."

A tall man in a flat cap and tweed jacket was tying a bundle of rather battered-looking tools together. As Mandy went up to him, something caught her eye. There, on top of the piano, was Frisky's cage.

Mandy gave a shout and leaped up on the

stage. "Frisky!" She had thought he would be fast asleep but all the hustle and bustle must have woken him up. He was sitting by his food bowl.

Mandy beamed at him through the bars of the cage. "Oh, Frisky, I'm *so* pleased to see you! Are you all right?"

Frisky twitched his nose then went on eating. He looked perfectly well; perky as anything and stuffing his cheek pouches full of food. He seemed none the worse for his journey round Welford.

"He's fine," a deep voice said from behind her. "You must be Mandy?"

Mandy turned to see Mr Jenkins smiling at her.

"Oh, Mr Jenkins," said Mandy. "I've been so worried about him."

"I know," Mr Jenkins said. "I'm really sorry. When I picked up the jumble I thought the cage was empty."

"I thought that's what had happened." James put his finger through the bars to tickle Frisky under the chin.

"People give all sorts of things to jumble

sales. I just thought maybe someone had lost a hamster and was giving away the cage."

"It doesn't matter," Mandy said. "He's safe and sound, that's the main thing."

"When did you find him?" James asked.

"I'd unloaded all the stuff," Mr Jenkins told them, "and was just going to lock up when I heard a strange noise. I'll tell you, it gave me quite a scare."

Mandy frowned. "What do you mean?"

"Well," Mr Jenkins raised his eyebrows. "It was a squeak, squeak . . . I thought it was a ghost!"

Mandy and James burst out laughing.

Mr Jenkins was laughing too.

"What did you do?" Mandy asked.

"Well, I tracked the noise down to a pile of old curtains," Mr Jenkins said. "Then, when I moved them aside, there was the hamster cage with this little chap running inside his wheel like a maniac. I was mighty relieved, I can tell you."

"I bet," James said.

"I was going to phone your gran," Mr Jenkins said. "But I'd promised my wife I'd take her to the pictures in Walton and she was ready when I got back. I'm sorry you were so worried, Mandy."

"It's OK," Mandy beamed him a smile. "As long as he's all right. He's not mine, you see. I've been looking after him for Gran's friend. He's been staying at Hamster Hotel."

It was Mr Jenkins's turn to look surprised. "Hamster Hotel?"

James chuckled. "Lilac Cottage," he explained.

"Oh," said Mr Jenkins. "I see." He looked a bit puzzled and Mandy didn't really think he saw at all.

Gran and Grandad arrived. They came to see Frisky, then went off to help sort out the jumble.

"Do you want to give me a hand?" Gran asked Mandy. "You could help Grandad with the books and magazines if you like, James."

"Right," James said.

"If there's one on dog training, you'd better buy it, James," Mandy called as she went to help Gran.

"Good idea." James began hunting through the pile.

Gran was sorting out a heap of old jumpers and cardigans.

"Hey," Mandy picked one up. "This looks like Grandad's old—"

But she got no further. Gran had snatched the jumper from her fingers. "Shh. He doesn't know," she whispered.

But it was too late. Grandad had seen it. He came rushing over faster than Mandy had ever seen him move before.

"Dorothy!" His voice was like thunder.

Gran was holding the jumper behind her back. "Yes, dear?" she said calmly.

"Dorothy!" Grandad was dodging about, trying to see behind her back. "That looks like . . ."

Everyone had stopped work and was watching.

"It is, Mr Hope," James called. "It's your gardening jumper." Then his hand flew to his mouth. He had given the game away.

Grandad held out his hand towards Gran. "Thank you, James. I'm glad us men stick

together. Give it to me, Dorothy," he
ordered sternly.

"It's full of holes," Gran said.

"I like them." Grandad was still holding
out his hand.

"It's faded," Gran said.

"I like it faded." Grandad tried to grab the
jumper.

"It . . . it . . . smells!" Gran backed away.

"I'll wash it," Grandad promised. "Anyway, it's a nice smell. Earthy . . ."

'It's, it's . . ." Gran couldn't think of anything else.

". . . it's Grandad's favourite jumper," Mandy finished for her.

"Oh, well, all right." Gran gave it to Grandad with a sigh. Everyone laughed and clapped.

Then Gran laughed too. She put her arms round Grandad and gave him a hug. "Oh, Tom, you'll be the death of me," she said wiping her eyes.

"Nonsense." Grandad gave her a loud kiss on the cheek.

"I've been hunting for my jumper everywhere," Grandad said to Mandy when Gran had gone back to sorting jumble. "I might have known your gran would try to pull a trick like that."

Mandy suddenly remembered how Grandad had spent ages looking through all the drawers and cupboards. So that's what he had been up to. She laughed and gave him a hug.

"Is it all right if we take Frisky home, now?" Mandy asked Grandad when all the jumble was sorted neatly into piles on the tables. It was almost lunch-time.

Grandad looked at his watch. "Yes, I'll run you home if you like. We don't want Frisky out in that cold air. We'll come back later for the sale." He glanced over to where Gran was talking to two of the ladies. "Who knows, I might even find myself another jumper with holes in."

Mandy and James chuckled. They said goodbye to everyone and put Frisky carefully in the car. Frisky hadn't been at all worried by the noise and bustle and had gone into his nest for a snooze.

Mandy felt excited as they travelled back to Lilac Cottage.

She just couldn't wait to show Frisky his adventure playground!

10

Farewell

On the way home they passed Mr Hope coming out of Animal Ark.

"Please stop, Grandad," Mandy said. "I *must* tell Dad about Frisky."

Grandad pulled up and she wound down her window.

Mr Hope laughed as he listened to her story.

"I don't know, Mandy," he said. "You do get into some scrapes."

"It wasn't *my* fault," Mandy said indignantly. "We've given Frisky the best care in the world."

"I know, Mandy," her dad said. "Well, we'll be pleased to see you back home. It's been really quiet without you," he added, teasing her.

"Is my bedroom finished?" Mandy asked. She had been looking forward to seeing it now it had been decorated.

"Yep." Mr Hope opened the boot of his car and put his bag inside. "It looks great. Lovely colour, although I expect you'll soon have all your posters up again and we won't be able to see much of the walls."

"I certainly will. See you later, Dad." Mandy wound the window up. "I'll have to get one of a hamster to remind me of Frisky," she said to James and Grandad.

"Me too," James said. "That's if I can find enough space on my wall."

Mr Hope waved as they set off again for Lilac Cottage.

Back indoors, they took Frisky up to the spare room.

"Here we are." Mandy put the cage on the table. "Home safe and sound."

James peered into the cage. "You know I don't think he really cares where he is as long as he's got a nice warm nest to curl up in."

"I bet he didn't like that cold old hall, all the same." Mandy picked up the little apple branch. "Come on, let's make his playground while he's asleep."

Mandy and James carefully fixed the branch inside the cage. They hung the cotton reels from one end.

"If we tie them close together he'll be able to jump over them," Mandy said.

They did that, then they put the ladders into position. Last of all they thoroughly cleaned out the cage and filled Frisky's food bowl and water bottle.

"There," Mandy said when they had finished. "All spick and span for tomorrow."

"Tomorrow?" James said.

"He's going home," Mandy told him sadly.

"Oh," said James. "That's our holiday over, then. We haven't done much training with Blackie, have we?"

"Not really," Mandy said. "We could do some this afternoon if you like."

James bit his lip. "I think I'd rather help out at the jumble sale."

Mandy grinned. "Me too."

The following day, Mandy woke up to a strange noise. She sat up, stretched and yawned. She had oiled Frisky's wheel again so it couldn't be that.

Then she saw what it was. Frisky was racing up and down his ladders, along his apple branch and over and over his cotton reels. He was having the time of his life.

Mandy gave a little cry of delight and jumped out of bed. She sat and watched him race round and round. Eventually he stopped and took a drink from his water bottle. Then he sat washing his face. After that he just stared at Mandy for a minute or two, his little nose twitching. It was almost as if he was saying 'thank you'.

Mandy waggled her finger through the bars.

"Now you behave yourself when you get back home," she said. She opened the door and picked him up. He ran up her arm then sat on her shoulder. Mandy could see him in the mirror. He looked so bright and perky. She felt proud that she and James had looked after him so well.

She let Frisky run around a bit then put him back in his cage. "I've got to pack my bag, Frisky," she told him. "I'm going home today, too."

Mandy dressed and packed her bag. She took it downstairs. Gran and Grandad were sitting at the kitchen table.

"Home today, then?" Grandad looked up from the Sunday paper.

"Yes." Mandy sat down and helped herself to cereal. "I'm really going to miss Frisky."

"He'll miss you too, I'm sure," Gran said. She was counting the money taken at the jumble sale. "I don't suppose he's ever had so much luxury."

Mandy smiled. "He loves his adventure playground."

"Good," Gran said. "It'll be something for him to remember his holiday by."

"That's what we thought." Mandy still sounded sad.

Grandad folded up his paper. "Well, I'd better go and dig those potatoes for lunch. You staying, Mandy?"

Mandy bit her lip. She *wanted* to stay with Frisky as long as possible but she wanted to get home too. She was beginning to miss it and she was dying to see her bedroom.

Gran sat back looking pleased. "Over two hundred pounds!" she said. "That'll help with the funds for the new church roof." She looked at Grandad over the top of her glasses. "There would have been an extra fifty pence if you'd have let me sell your jumper, Tom."

Grandad gave a grunt and fumbled in his pocket. He took out a fifty-pence piece and gave it to Gran. "Oh, here you are, then." His eyes twinkled.

Gran took it and put it in the bag with the

rest of the money. "Thanks, Tom."

"When is Frisky's owner coming for him?" Mandy asked.

"This morning," Gran said. "They actually got back late last night so I should think she'll be here quite soon."

"She'll have missed Frisky, I expect," Mandy said.

"I'm sure she will. But she'll be ever so pleased he's been well looked after." Gran put her arm round Mandy. "I'm really grateful for your help, Mandy."

"It's OK, Gran."

Mandy suddenly thought of all the things she had got to do that day. She had promised to go for a walk with James and Blackie to look for conkers in Monkton Spinney. She wanted to put her books back into their bookcase and stick her posters back up on her bedroom wall. And she and James were going to read the dog training book James had got at the sale. It might have some handy hints on what to do with Blackie.

Mandy looked at her Gran. "Would it be

all right if I went home straight after break-fast?"

"Of course it would," Gran said. "Go when you like. You know you can come back any time."

"Thanks, Gran." Mandy hurriedly finished her toast then went upstairs again. Frisky was sitting on his branch. He looked a bit sleepy now.

Mandy peered through the bars. "Bye, Frisky." There was a little catch in her voice. "I hope you've enjoyed your holi-day." She took him out for one last time and stroked him gently. Then, seeing how sleepy he was, she put him carefully back inside. He scrambled up to his little plat-form, turned and gazed at her for a minute. His whiskers twitched. Then he climbed into his nest. Soon all Mandy could see was a tight little ball of fur.

Outside, the early morning mist had cleared and the sun was shining. It was going to be a lovely autumn day. Mandy ran down the hill and along past the green. The front door of Animal Ark was open and Mrs Hope was just coming out.

"Mum!" Mandy shouted and ran up the path to meet her.

Mrs Hope gave her a hug. "Mandy! I was just going to walk up to the cottage to meet you."

"I couldn't wait to get back," said Mandy. "How's everything? How's the chinchilla?"

"He's fine. Everything's fine."

Mandy and her mum went indoors. The smell of fresh paint greeted Mandy as she ran up the stairs and burst in through her

bedroom door. She drew in her breath. It looked beautiful. Clean and fresh and bright.

Mandy sat on the bed. She thought about Frisky, all curled up snug in his little nest. She hoped he would be pleased to be going home too.

Just then her mum called from the bottom of the stairs. "Mandy, we've got a badger cub someone's brought in. Come down and see him."

Mandy leaped up. How brilliant! She had never seen a badger cub close up. She ran downstairs to join her mum.

There was no doubt about it, it had been fun staying at Hamster Hotel, but Animal Ark was the best!